ZOO TRIP!

Written by
Quentin Flynn

Illustrated by
Peter Townsend

HORWITZ
MARTIN
EDUCATION

Contents

Chapter 1

Feeding Time

"Who ate the last of the blueberries?" growled Yokie.

The great brown grizzly bear glared at his brother and sister, who were busily searching through the long grass for the last morsels of their breakfast. The zookeeper never seemed to bring enough berries to satisfy the three large bears.

"It's not fair. I was saving them," cried Yokie, sniffing towards the other two bears to see if he could smell blueberries on their beary breath. "And now they're gone!"

Grunting angrily, the other two bears moved out of Yokie's way.

"First in, first served," growled Yokie's brother, Tor. "Anyway, what's the point of saving them? They'll only get squashed and turn rotten."

"You can't blame us," added his sister, Shoah. "You know that blueberries are only in season for a few weeks. You were just too slow."

Yokie sighed. Feeding time at the zoo was always a trial, especially when you shared an enclosure with two other hungry bears. Now there was nothing left to look forward to for the rest of the day. Until dinnertime, of course, thought Yokie lazily.

Dinnertime was almost as good as breakfast. He just wished there weren't so many hours in between. There was nothing to do except sleep and squint at the silly humans wandering past.

Yokie, Tor and Shoah had learnt that humans liked
nothing more than to point their cameras at them
in hope of the perfect photograph. So, just to
annoy them, especially the small ones, each bear
had a perfect
hiding place within
the enclosure.

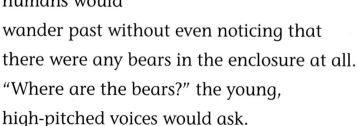

Hiding all day meant
they could sleep quite
happily without
being disturbed by
the constant whirring
and clicking and
flashing of the
cameras. It also
meant that most
humans would
wander past without even noticing that
there were any bears in the enclosure at all.
"Where are the bears?" the young,
high-pitched voices would ask.

"I don't know," would come the older humans' lower-pitched reply.

"Over here, dummy!" Yokie and his brother and sister would snigger to themselves. "Yoo hoo!" Nothing was quite so satisfying as disappointing humans. Nothing except breakfast and dinner, that is.

Yokie was determined to be first when the keeper brought in the tray of food for dinner. He was going to get all the blueberries this time, even if it meant having to fight with Tor and Shoah. But for the time being, there was nothing else to do except sleep away the day.

"Ready for sleep?" Yokie asked gruffly.

"Uh-huh," replied his brother and sister. And with that, all three slumped to the ground, flattened their huge bodies out amongst the tall grass and rocks, and closed their eyes. Not even an ear or a whisker poked out from above the grass. They were safely hidden from all prying human eyes.

All around the zoo, animals from Africa, North and South America, Australia, Asia and Europe had the same idea — feeding time was over for the morning, and it was time to settle down and hide from the clicking, flashing cameras. Nothing else would happen until dinner time. Nothing else of interest ever did.

The younger animals just cuddled up to the older ones, and as their eyelids grew heavy, they listened to stories of the old days, and far off countries. All around the zoo, young animals drifted off to sleep to the sound of tall tales about adventure and excitement. Little did they know that the day would turn out to be very different than usual — and that they would end up with a new tale to tell in the years to come!

Chapter 2

The Wild Snake Eater

"I don't believe it," said Kickback in amazement. Her jaw dropped down, and her eyes widened. She stopped scratching her pouch and stood at the rear of her enclosure with a stunned look on her face. "It can't be!"

She lifted her nose high in the air, and twitched it furiously, trying to sniff that scent again. Flicking her ears back and forth, she tried to catch a snatch of the voice she had just heard drifting across the kangaroo enclosure.

A faint human voice floated across the enclosure.

"I can hear 'em. Listen! You can just hear them scratching their pouches with their front paws!"

Kickback quickly whirled around, rudely hissing at the other kangaroos.

"Shh!" she said. "Stop scratching." The other kangaroos looked quite stunned. What was wrong with scratching?

Kickback cautiously craned her neck above the long grass, trying to make out where the voice was coming from. Quickly she withdrew her head.

"I think one of the small humans saw me," she said nervously. "But I caught a glimpse of the big one. "I'm just not sure if it's him, or not!"

At this, the other kangaroos grew interested. "Who?" they whispered, wondering whether to peek over the top of the grass at the group of humans Kickback had seen.

"SHHH!" said Kickback forcefully. "Listen!"

The human voice began again. "Once, in the outback of Australia, when I'd finished my job as a crocodile wrestler, I worked as a kangaroo jockey."

Kickback looked startled as the voice continued.

"For days, I hitched rides with camel drivers, travelling deeper and deeper into the desert. Finally, I arrived at the town of Boolydooly, where the kangaroo races were about to begin."

Kickback almost fainted with excitement which, for a kangaroo, was a very unusual thing.

"Boolydooly," she repeated breathlessly. "It IS him! Now I know for sure!"

"WHO?" demanded the other kangaroos in voices that were bound to be overheard by the humans, poor as their hearing usually was.

Kickback turned to face the small herd. They waited for her to speak. An odd look had come over her face, and she was shaking her head in disbelief.

"The Wild Snake Eater from Zanzibar!" she replied softly. A shiver of excitement buzzed through the kangaroos. Suddenly, the atmosphere became electric.

"The Wild Snake Eater? You mean he's real? I thought that was just a story," said one of the young bucks, blinking rapidly.

"Oh, no," replied Kickback, with a quiver in her voice. "He's real, alright. If he wasn't, our great-great-great grandfather, Big Red, would have ended up as mincemeat in Mad Butcher-Bob's shop many years ago. And we," said Kickback matter-of-factly, "would never have been born."

Every kangaroo in the enclosure knew the story of the Wild Snake Eater from Zanzibar. They had heard it told and retold ever since they were tiny joeys in their mothers' pouches.

The story always began, "Out in the desert plains of Boolydooly, we once roamed wild — thousands upon thousands of kangaroos, just like you and me."

The storyteller would then drop their voice, as they introduced evil Butcher-Bob Mackenzie.

"Then one day, the man we knew as Mad Butcher-Bob arrived in town."

The young joeys would shiver and quake in their pouches. They all knew what Butcher-Bob Mackenzie did for a living.

"Mad Butcher-Bob had a plan to become the biggest hamburger patty supplier in the whole world. But he wasn't going to use beef for his hamburger patties. As Butcher-Bob would say, 'cattle costs cash.' He was going to use *kangaroo meat* for his hamburger patties!"

At this point in the story, most of the younger joeys burrowed deep into their pouches, and covered their ears. Only the older ones were brave enough to continue listening.

"Butcher-Bob would hold kangaroo races every Wednesday," so the story went. "And those kangaroos who didn't win, ended up on top of a slice of lettuce, between two buns. That is, until the day the Wild Snake Eater turned up at the races!"

At this news, the joeys and kangaroos would cheer wildly. They loved this part of the story.

"The Wild Snake Eater spoke the secret language
of the kangaroos from Cape Wotchitywitchity.
He rode your great-great-great grandfather, Big Red,
to victory against Butcher-Bob. When Butcher-Bob
was in a huff at losing, and threatened to turn ALL
the kangaroos into mincemeat, even the winners —
there was big trouble!"

"That's when the Wild Snake Eater threatened to tell everyone what was really in those hamburger patties. Butcher-Bob was so alarmed that he let all the kangaroos go — and they followed Big Red and the Wild Snake Eater from Zanzibar off into the red desert."

"The news spread, like wildfire, all over Australia about the human who had saved so many of us. His description, the way he smelt and the way he talked has been passed down from generation to generation."

"And that," boomed Kickback, returning the kangaroos in the enclosure back to reality, "is how I know that this human — " she pointed towards the wire fence, " — is the Wild Snake Eater from Zanzibar!"

Having told her story, Kickback couldn't contain herself any longer. She poked her head above the grass and stared at the humans. Her two ears twitched, flicking backwards and forwards.

"Look!" said one of the small humans next to the Wild Snake Eater.

Kickback excitedly let out a low, booming sound and thumped the ground with her tail. Slowly, all the kangaroos in the enclosure poked their heads above the long grass to stare at this famous hero.

Suddenly, a strange clicking language floated towards them. "Tch, tch, tch, tch." The kangaroos recognised it immediately. The language of Wotchitywitchitese! Now, there could be no doubt. Every kangaroo bounded towards the fence, hoping for a better look at their hero!

Young and old, the kangaroos twittered, chattered and thumped their tails, bouncing around in excitement.

As the Wild Snake Eater from Zanzibar waved cheerily at the kangaroos, Kickback almost fainted.

"He waved at us! He waved at us!" she chattered noisily. "What a day! What excitement. I think I shall have to lie down!"

And with that, she did faint. Which, for a kangaroo, was a very unusual thing to do.

Chapter **3**

The Prisoner Of Zortan

Yokie flattened out a nice patch of grass amongst the tall blades at the rear of the bear enclosure, and happily dozed in the warm sunshine.
He ignored the flies that were mindlessly buzzing around as, half-asleep, he dreamed of a huge bowl of blueberries.

But, slowly the bear began to stir as a familiar sounding voice drifted across the enclosure.

"It was so cold that winter, the ice covering the lake was ten metres thick. The snowfalls were so heavy that by the time you took one foot off the ground to take another step, the falling snow had covered your footprint completely!"

Something stirred in Yokie's sleepy brain. He dragged his thoughts away from blueberries and tried to concentrate on what he had just heard. Who else had told him a story like that?

The human voice continued. "One morning, I went out to check my letterbox. It was at the end of our road so the postie didn't have to travel along a sometimes treacherous road. When I returned, the log cabin I'd built out of tree trunks had disappeared. Completely covered in snow, I suppose!"

Yokie flicked his ears, and lazily opened one eye. This story sounded strangely familiar. A long-forgotten memory started to form in his mind. He remembered being a tiny bear cub, snuggled up close to his mother. A contented bear-smile spread across his grizzly face at the thought, as he once again listened to the voice.

"Well, there was nothing else to do but to try and find some shelter. Eventually, I found a nice warm cave, and headed inside. Imagine my surprise when I discovered I was standing on a piece of thick, warm carpet!"

Like a thunderbolt, the full memory of those long-lost bear cub days flashed through Yokie's mind. Startled, he opened both eyes. Someone out there, beyond the stone fence, was telling the same story that he had heard from his mother, years and years before. The story of the Prisoner of Zortan!

How could anyone else — let alone a human —
know the story that had been passed down
through his family for three generations? Unless ...
could it be possible?

Yokie was now fully awake and his ears strained
to hear the voice.

"Shoah! Tor!" he whispered urgently to his brother and sister.

"I didn't eat your blueberries," grumbled Shoah sleepily.

"Neither did I," yawned his brother, Tor.

"Shh!" said Yokie under his breath. "Do either of you remember the story about the Prisoner of Zortan?"

"You mean the fairy tale about the strange human who saved the lives of our great-grandmother and her cubs," groaned Shoah dreamily. "Yes, I remember. Mum was always good at telling tall stories to send us to sleep."

"What was it about again?" asked Tor, who was never very good at remembering stories or jokes or birthdays.

Tor curled up in the grass and pretended to be
a tiny cub again, as Yokie's hushed voice quickly
retold their mother's tale.

"Our great-grandmother and her cubs — including
our grandad, when he was only a few months old
— were hibernating in the family cave over winter.
It was a terrible, harsh, freezing winter like no-one
had ever seen before."

"Suddenly, something — or someone — flopped down on top of them, waking them all up. Imagine their surprise when they opened their eyes to stare straight into a pair of ... human eyes!"

Tor and Shoah grunted happily as Yokie continued retelling the story.

"Great-grandmother was trying to decide whether she should finish off the human with a swipe of her razor-sharp claws, or whether she should just go back to sleep, when a terrible commotion broke out at the cave entrance."

"Old Yellowtooth, the most ferocious, bad-tempered grizzly that ever lived in the Yukon, was on the rampage. He'd woken up, starving, and was going to eat whatever he found in their cave, whether it was bear or not!"

"Great-grandmother was terrified. There was no way that she would be able to fight off an angry male grizzly — especially one as mean and vicious as Old Yellowtooth."

"Just as all hope was lost, the crazy human leapt up and ..."

But Yokie didn't have time to finish his sentence. From beyond the stone wall at the front of the enclosure came a deep, rumbling ROAR that rattled every bone in his body. Yokie shivered with excitement.

He had first heard that roar when his mother had acted out the sound the human had made. He knew that roar off by heart.

Now, he was certain! His black nose and furry head shot up to stare at the human behind the wall. No-one else knew that story, he was sure of it! No-one, of course, except the human ... the fabled Prisoner of Zortan!

With a loud grunt, Yokie dragged his huge, lumbering body up, up, up into the air until he was standing at full height on his powerful back legs. It *was* the Prisoner of Zortan! It *had* to be!

The figure waved at Yokie, who dropped back down on all fours. By now, Shoah and Tor were wide awake and stared in surprise at Yokie.

"Is it him?" they asked. "The Prisoner of Zortan?"

"You've heard the story," replied Yokie, shaking his head in amazement. "After spending all winter in the cave with him, great-grandmother and her cubs could describe the Prisoner of Zortan in every detail. With a little more hair, and a brown beard, that human out there matches the description exactly!"

"I'm going to look," said Tor excitedly.

"Me, too!" said Shoah, staring down her nose at the humans.

With surprising speed, the three grizzly bears loped towards the stone fence, grinning.

"Are you really the Prisoner of Zortan?" they all roared together.

"Well, I'm certainly not Old Yellowtooth!" roared the human back at them.

At that, the three bears were speechless. They stared at the Prisoner of Zortan and he stared back at them, smiling and scratching his beard.

Yokie tried hard to think of something clever to say to the Prisoner of Zortan. He had never met a real-life hero before — especially one who had saved the lives of his great-grandmother and his grandfather.

But the only thing that popped into his head was, "Do you like blueberries?"

The Prisoner of Zortan just smiled and waved at the bears, and they watched in silence as he walked off, accompanied by three small human cubs. Shoah giggled.

"Couldn't you think of anything more sensible to say?" she snorted, in between the giggles. Tor started to laugh, too.

"Do you like blueberries?" he chortled, imitating his big brother. "Of all the things to ask the famous Prisoner of Zortan, you had to ask him *that?*"

Shoah and Tor rolled on the grass, helpless with laughter, causing the other animals in the zoo to wonder what was going on.

"What's so funny?" called out the giraffes.

"What's the big joke?" cackled the tropical birds.

"What's everyone laughing at?" howled the wolves.

"Wait till you hear this!" roared out Tor, in between gales of laughter.

Chapter **4**

The Siberian Tiger Tamer

As soon as they heard the news, the wolves were buzzing with life. They jostled with each other at the stone wall, jumping higher to get a better view from their enclosure.

"You know who the Prisoner of Zortan is, don't you," they barked to each other excitedly. "It's the human we know as the Siberian Tiger Tamer!"

The giraffes paraded like royalty, looking down their long necks at the human. They too started whispering to each other about a story they had heard somewhere before.

"The wolves call him the Siberian Tiger Tamer. We giraffes know him as 'The Nose' — the only human able to track polar bears through the Arctic night using his sense of smell!"

Soon, the whole zoo was buzzing with the news. Every animal knew this human from long-forgotten stories, tales, and legends. Every animal craned their neck to get a better glimpse of their hero.

The wolves could hardly contain their excitement as the man they knew as the Siberian Tiger Tamer stopped outside their enclosure.

"He floated down from the sky," yelped the older wolves to the younger cubs. "This was a time when your ancestors used to roam around the dark forests of Bulgaria, hunting small animals and eating the humans' sheep and goats. And do you know what he brought with him?"

Of course, every wolf, old and young, knew exactly what the Siberian Tiger Tamer had brought with him. The most delectable, delicious delicacy ever tasted in wolfdom.

"Yellow Squiggly Corn-Snacks!" they all barked and bayed and yelped in excitement. Then, they all started drooling at the thought of these legendary treats.

Even though most of the wolves had never tasted a yellow squiggly corn-snack before, the stories they had heard made them drool and shake excitedly. In the wolf world, believe it or not, there was simply nothing that tasted as good as a yellow squiggly corn-snack!

The Siberian Tiger Tamer leant closer to the stone wall and, to the surprise of every creature within hearing distance, spoke to them.

"I've only got half a packet of yellow corn-snack squiggles! So you'll all have to share, OK?"

The wolves nodded greedily, jumping and jostling even more, as the Siberian Tiger Tamer reached

into his pocket and pulled out a half-eaten packet of squiggles.

"Over here! Over here!" they all howled, as the Siberian Tiger Tamer took a handful of yellow corn-snack squiggles out of the packet and flicked them over the wall. They soared through the air, causing ten wolves to dive for them at once.

The wolves almost went crazy with delight, as the delicious taste of corn-snacks melted in their mouths. They had never tasted anything like it! All the stories were true! This was simply the best-tasting food on the planet!

The Siberian Tiger Tamer grinned as the wolves behind the wall howled for more. He flicked and flicked squiggles through the air until the packet was empty. Luckily, every wolf was able to taste at least one of the corn-snacks, and all agreed that there was just nothing that could compare to this delectable taste.

The Siberian Tiger Tamer grinned again as he started talking to the small human cubs who stood beside him.

"Lucky things!" howled the wolves.

"I bet they're able to eat all the yellow squiggly corn-snacks they want!"

"He's leaving! He's leaving!" called out all the animals.

"Come back soon!" yelled out all the animals.

The man that some knew as the Wild Snake Eater, or the Prisoner of Zortan, or the Siberian Tiger Tamer, or a dozen other names was leaving. As a farewell gesture, he held out his arms to the many animals that crowded the fences along the pathway.

"Three cheers from all the animals!" called out the giraffes.

Suddenly, without warning, the whole zoo erupted into an explosion of shrieks and grunts and hoots and squeaks and cries and screams and roars.

Gradually, as the humans disappeared into the distance, animals in every enclosure and cage settled down to tell their favourite old stories, which had been passed down from generation to generation.

And the younger animals sat there listening and trying to remember every detail.

For all the animals knew that one day, when they had cubs or joeys or pups or kittens of their own, the human hero would return. Once more then, the stories would be passed on to new generations of animals, to be told and retold, time and time again.